TINY HANDS

Spring

Creative Activities for Young Children

BARRON'S

Original title of the book in Spanish: *Manitas: Primavera*
© Copyright Parramón Ediciones, S.A., 1997—World Rights
Published by Parramón Ediciones, S.A., Barcelona, Spain

Author: Parramón's Editorial Team
Text and Exercises: Anna Galera Bassachs, Mònica Martí I Garbayo, and Isabel Sanz Muelas
Illustrators: Parramón's Editorial Team
Photographs: Estudio Nos y Soto, AGE Fotostock, Incolor, Fototeca Stone

© Copyright of English edition for the United States, Canada, its territories and possessions by
Barron's Educational Series, Inc., 1999.

All inquiries should be addressed to:
Barron's Educational Series, Inc.
250 Wireless Boulevard
Hauppauge, New York 11788
http://www.barronseduc.com

Library of Congress Catalog Card No.: 98-72536
International Standard Book No.: 0-7641-0743-7

Printed in Spain
9 8 7 6 5 4 3 2 1

CONTENTS

4
Introduction

5
Techniques Used

6
Methodology

7
How the Book Is Organized

7
Spring

8
Caterpillar
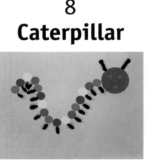

10
Flower Cart

12
Clay Necklace

14
Spring Landscape
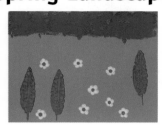

16
Ladybug 1

18
Butterfly

20
Flowers

22
Two Butterflies
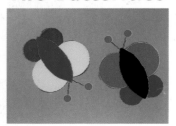

24
Stamped Painting
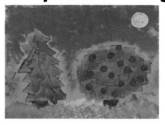

26
Bean Flower

28
Ladybug 2
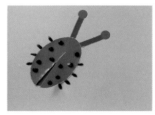

30
Yellow Butterfly

32
Tulip

34
Yarn Butterfly
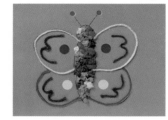

36
Ant

38
Gift Box with Flower

40
Wall Tile with Flower

42
Templates

INTRODUCTION

The three teachers who wrote this book specialize in early childhood education. They work with children of three, four, and five years old, respectively. Because they could not find material for the age groups they were teaching, they decided to compile a book containing a series of activities designed to foster artistic expression and creativity in children.
This book provides adults with ideas and strategies for directing each activity so that children can carry them out with the greatest independence—playing, experimenting, and fully enjoying various techniques, thereby progressively acquiring skills and self-sufficiency.

Creative Expression in Preschoolers

Children in this age group have a great deal of curiosity and a desire to discover everything around them. Their thought processes are based on meaningful learning—comprehensive learning that allows children to relate what they already know to new information they are learning. This type of learning allows children to get to know and interpret, use and evaluate their surroundings.

In order to promote this process, the activities in this book have a global focus. Why do we use a global focus? Children cannot separate the parts from the whole and cannot take a single piece of information out of its context,
but, rather, perceive various stimuli and sensations at once.

The teacher must have different tools and strategies available to relate each handcrafted piece with the various parts of the curriculum. At the end of each activity, therefore, we provide guidelines to help globalize the activity. When carrying out activities, the teacher must not forget the importance of seeing that the children practice habits of cleanliness, neatness, and personal hygiene, reinforcing their sense of independence.

Cognitive activity through direct observation—such as the handling of objects and
experimentation—must be stimulated at this stage. The activities presented here allow children to gain knowledge through discovery.

Artistic creativity is a part of all educational processes and is found in all daily activities and situations. Art is an excellent medium of expression. The various works created by children can provide a great deal of information about them.

—Anna Galera Bassachs, Mònica Martí i Garbayo, and Isabel Sanz Muelas

Techniques Used

The different techniques to be found in this book, listed below, are those best suited and most commonly used for this age group.

Hole punching: You need a felt pad and an awl or fine hole puncher. A series of consecutive holes must be punched along previously drawn lines in order to punch out the desired figure, without tearing the paper with the awl or hole puncher or ripping the paper with your fingers.

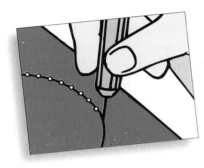

Cutting: Hold the scissors correctly in one hand while holding the paper with the other. Move the paper along with the scissors and follow the outlines.

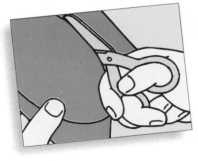

Gluing: Use only the amount of glue needed for the surfaces to be glued. If the area is large, spread the glue on the paper and simply place the cut-out pieces on top. If it is small, place the piece to be pasted on the gluestick and spread it with glue, then paste it onto the paper.

Tearing using fingers: This should be done slowly and carefully, pinching the paper between your fingers.

Modeling with plasticine: To cover a flat surface, take a pinch of clay and spread it with your thumb. Some pressure will be required to make the plasticine stick to the surface of the oaktag. Whenever you use plasticine, it should always be varnished afterward to fix it in place and make it shiny and hard.

Modeling with clay: The clay must be kneaded well before using it to remove any air bubbles and avoid possible cracks later. It is important to wet the clay with water when joining separate pieces, getting rid of cracks and giving a smooth finish. It is a good idea to paint or varnish the piece once it has dried to give it a smoother finish.

Painting: Use wax crayons or clay, and fingers, hands, or paintbrushes. When using a paintbrush, remove any excess water to avoid dripping and lumps.

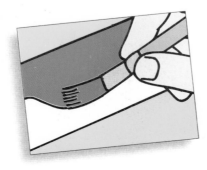

Making stamps: Stamps can be made of various materials (potatoes, sponges, corks, fingers, hands, and so on). The best way to cover these stamps in paint is to soak a sponge in a wide dish containing watered-down paint.

Making collages: Various materials can be used (cloth, paper in different colors and textures, stickers in different colors and shapes, wool, toothpicks, beans, pasta, coffee, and so on).

Covering holes with transparent materials: Waxed paper or cellophane wrap can be used. The glue must always be spread on the back around the hole in the oaktag to avoid staining or wrinkling the cellophane or paper.

Making balls: Balls can be made with tissue paper. Tear a piece of tissue paper and wrinkle it into a ball with your fingertips. This technique exercises the children's fine motor skills by making them pinch with their fingertips (using their index finger and thumb). When gluing, spread the glue on the surface of the oaktag and then stick the balls on. If the ball is very small, put the glue directly on the ball instead of on the oaktag.

Methodology

The methodology presented here, based on the authors' professional experience, is useful for directing artistic activities in the classroom with children of this age group.

The most important factor will be organizing the classroom and planning the activity and the materials. You, the teacher, will have to know exactly which materials will be necessary for each session and what procedure should be followed to direct the children in each activity.

Before beginning to work with the material and carry out the tasks, the children should understand what they are about to do and why, in order to motivate them and catch their interest. They should be encouraged and each theme should be placed in context in order to attain the desired educational goals. They should understand that everything they do has a purpose and can be used in other situations, that the work to be carried out is not an isolated activity but forms part of the real world. That is why the activities have a global focus; therefore, stress how the activity relates to the real world before beginning it.

Once the children's curiosity and desire to discover new things have been awakened, you can show them what the finished piece (which you will have already made as an example) will look like.

To achieve positive results, it is important to choose the right time for the activity and spread it out over more than one sitting. At this age, children tire quickly of doing the same thing for too long; therefore, depending on duration and complexity, the activity will have to be spread out over several class sessions in order to be more relaxing and fun.

It is recommended that the activity be done first thing in the morning or afternoon, when the children are more receptive, relaxed, and rested. The interests and moods of the children must be seriously considered before starting the activity. If you see that they are restless and cannot concentrate, you may want to put it off until another time. You should avoid making the mistake of forcing the situation, since then children would not really enjoy the activity and the results would not be so positive.

Depending on the number of children in the class and on their personalities (restless, receptive, relaxed), on the difficulty of the technique being used, or if it is the first time it has been introduced, you should either work with the entire class at one time or with small groups. In each exercise, you will find some guidelines that should be followed when teaching all of the children at once or in small groups.

When you are working with a small group, the rest of the class should be involved in some activity that does not require adult help, so that you can fully concentrate on teaching the group.

On the other hand, when working with the entire class, the activity will probably be more guided; therefore, the most important factor will be knowing how to keep their attention. The children will have to listen closely to your instructions in order to correctly carry out the activity.

Participating too actively in the children's work should be avoided, as this reduces their independence. Do not be too preoccupied with a piece's perfection; make sure that the children play and experiment with the different techniques and materials, fully enjoying them.

If it is an activity the children can do alone, it will not be necessary to guide them too much, even when working with the class as a whole. The important thing is to allow them to express themselves freely. Allow them their creativity.

If the materials to be used are very specific, these should be handed out to each child. If not, place a container in the middle of each table so the materials are easily accessible to everyone. This will help the children learn to share.

Once the class is finished, it is important to have the children realize that they must clean and put away their work utensils, as well as take care of their personal hygiene. During class, they must treat the tools and materials respectfully.

The majority of the techniques presented throughout this book can be modified to suit the children's level; for instance, if an activity calls for punching techniques, cutting can be substituted if the children are older, and so on. By the same token, the basic idea can be used, but with different techniques according to your own creativity and personal motivation and the materials available.

This book was designed to serve as a practical work tool, since it is based on the real-life experiences of three elementary school teachers. We hope their guidelines and advice will make your teaching easier and more diverse in the area of artistic expression. The presentation of each activity will help make the work more pleasant and fun so you and the children can fully enjoy it.

How the Book Is Organized

This book is organized to take into account the different ages of the children in this grade. The activities are classified according to their degree of difficulty. The classification is made according to classroom experience. All of these activities have been tested in the classroom on children in this age group. It should be noted, however, that these classifications are only intended to get you started, since we are dealing with open suggestions for activities that can be modified to suit the specific needs of each group; the same activity could be modified for different age groups by making it more or less complex.

Included are both two- and three-dimensional projects. Each activity includes a list of materials needed, the degree of difficulty (from one to three), guidelines for the teacher (how to do it), steps to follow divided into sessions, and some advice on how to make everything run more smoothly.

Each step is accompanied by a photograph or an illustration to facilitate comprehension.

Spring

For this season we offer a series of manual activities that relate to this season, a time rich in colors and changes in landscape, in which insects and flowers play the principal roles.

These activities will doubtless serve to broaden the resources that every teacher already has, but that may not be sufficient. The book can be used to work on themes related to nature and the most relevant occurrences of the season. At the same time, it will provide ideas for decorating album covers, making mobiles to hang in the classroom, and other projects.

1 CATERPILLAR

What materials are needed?

- *Blue oaktag*
- *Blue glossy paper*
- *Black plasticine*
- *Colored stickers: for each child, two small green circles, one small red triangle, and various large circles of different colors*
- *Awl and felt pad*
- *Glue stick*
- *Varnish and paintbrush*

How can the activity be done?

This activity can be done in three sessions of approximately half an hour each, working with the entire class at one time, since the activity can be easily supervised.

Session 1

For each child, prepare:
- *A sheet of blue oaktag with a wavy line already drawn on it*
- *A sheet of blue glossy paper with the circle for the head already drawn on it and ready to be punched out*
- *Colored stickers for the eyes and mouth*
- *Awl and felt pad*

1 **From the glossy paper, punch out the circle that will become the head.**

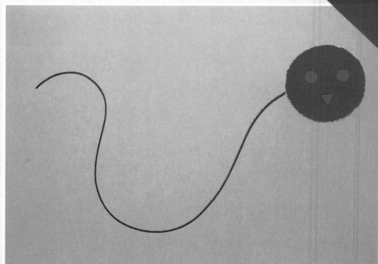

2 **Glue the head onto the upper end of the line on the oaktag and press the stickers down to make the face.**

Which techniques will be practiced?

- *Modeling with clay*
- *Punching out figures with an awl* • *Using colored stickers*

Session 2

For each table, prepare:
- *A tray containing enough of the large round stickers in the desired colors for all the children.*

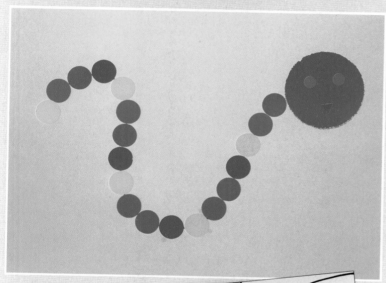

3 **Put the colored stickers along the line on the oaktag to make the caterpillar's body.**

Teaching Suggestions

- *Use this creative activity to demonstrate a **color series**.*
- *Work on the colors. This could be done in the form of a supervised activity, where the teacher would place a tray containing the different-colored stickers and then give a **color dictation**, telling the children which color to choose.*
- *The children can also be allowed to choose and stick on the colors **freely**, but without placing them too close together (overlapping) or too far apart.*
- *Review facial features when you have the children make the face of the caterpillar with the stickers.*

Session 3

For each child, prepare:
- *A piece of black plasticine*
- *Varnish and paintbrush*

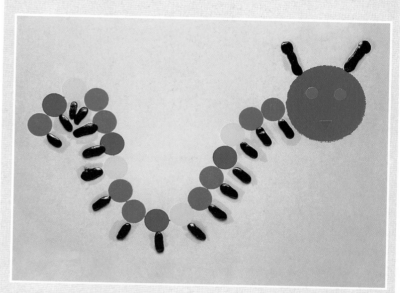

4 **Shape the black plasticine into the legs and antennas. Stick them onto the oaktag with some pressure so they don't fall off; then varnish everything.**

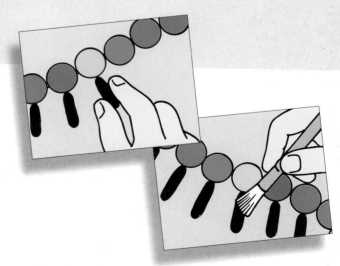

Practical Advice

- ***Plasticine:*** *It is better not to give out too much plasticine to each child so the children do not make the body parts too big.*

2 FLOWER CART

What materials are needed?

- Green oaktag
- Glossy paper in various colors
- Flat brown toothpicks
- Brown popsicle stick
- Round stickers in various colors and sizes
- Glue stick
- Awl and felt pad
- Template (see page 43)

How can the activity be done?

This activity can be done in three sessions of approximately half an hour each, working with the entire class at one time.

Session 1

For each table, prepare:
- *A tray containing some of the round stickers of different colors and sizes*
- *A tray containing some sheets of glossy paper of various colors, with flower outlines previously drawn on them*
- *A sheet of brown glossy paper with the wheel of the cart already drawn on it*
- *An awl and felt pad for each child*

1 Punch out the flowers and the wheel of the cart.

2 Place a round sticker in the center of each flower.

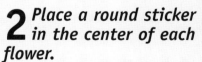

Practical Advice

- **Colored toothpicks:** *If brown toothpicks or popsicle sticks are not available, the children can color ordinary wooden ones with wax crayons, markers, or paint before gluing them on.*
- **Gluing toothpicks:** *When gluing the toothpicks, the children should pick them up by the tips and spread them with glue. This will require them to make an effort in order to pick up the toothpick and hold it correctly without it falling and without getting their fingers full of glue.*

Which techniques will be practiced?

Punching out shapes with an awl
Putting stickers on a surface and gluing paper and toothpicks

Session 2

For each table, prepare:
• A tray containing a sufficient amount of flat toothpicks
For each child, prepare:
• A sheet of green oaktag with the outline of the cart previously drawn on it
• A popsicle stick
• Glue

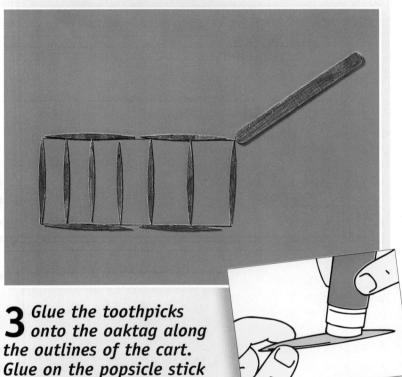

3 Glue the toothpicks onto the oaktag along the outlines of the cart. Glue on the popsicle stick to make the handle of the cart.

Session 3

For each child, prepare:
• The oaktag with toothpicks and popsicle stick already glued on it
• The punched-out flowers
• The punched-out wheel of the cart
• Glue

4 Glue the flowers onto the cart wherever you like, overlapping them somewhat. Glue the wheel into place.

Teaching Suggestions

Take this opportunity to talk with the children about carts—where they can be found, if you can see them in the street, what they are for, and so on.
Collect photographs and information about carts to complement the activity.

3 CLAY NECKLACE

What materials are needed?

- Clay
- String
- Pencil or stick
- Varnish or different colored paints and paintbrush

How can the activity be done?

This activity can be done in three sessions of approximately half an hour each (the last two sessions may end up being somewhat shorter), working with the entire class at one time.

Session 1

For each child, prepare:
- *A piece of clay*
- *A pencil or stick*
- *A tray on which to place the finished beads of the necklace*

1 **Take small pieces of clay and roll them into beads.**

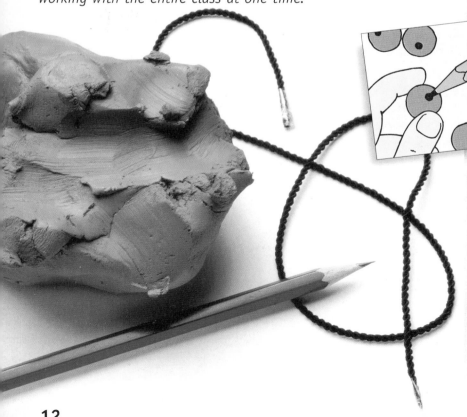

2 **As you make the beads, poke a hole through each one with the pencil or stick and leave it on the tray to dry.**

Which techniques will be practiced?

- *Modeling with clay* • *Poking holes with a pencil or stick*
- *Threading clay beads on a string*

Session 2

For each table, prepare:
- *A dish containing varnish*

For each child, you should prepare:
- *The tray containing the beads from the previous session, now dry*
- *A paintbrush*

3 Varnish or paint the clay beads and place them back in the tray to dry.

Session 3

For each child, prepare:
- *The tray containing the varnished or painted beads*
- *A string*

4 Thread all of the clay beads onto the string to form a necklace. Tie the ends in a knot.

Practical Advice

• **Modeling:** *Before the children begin modeling the beads, it is important that they first familiarize themselves with the material, playing with it freely for a while.*
• **Painting or varnishing:** *Once the necklace is finished, it can be painted. If the natural clay color is preferred, it is a good idea to varnish it to make the piece shine and be durable.*

Teaching Suggestions

- *Use this opportunity to discuss with the children what their* **perception of a necklace is**, *what it is for, who wears it, where you can buy it, what it can be made of, and so on.*
- *Discuss the* **properties of clay**: *color, texture, hard–soft.*

Single Session

Prepare a table in an art corner with:
• *Five trays, each containing a different color finger paint: blue, yellow, red, brown, and green*
• *Several tree leaves*
• *A sheet of green oaktag for each child*
• *A damp towel, rag, or paper towel for wiping hands*

What materials are needed?

• *Green oaktag*
• *Blue, red, yellow, green, and brown finger paint*
• *Leaves from trees*

How can the activity be done?

This activity can be done in a single session, working with small groups. Since the activity requires many paint colors and the children are to use them freely, the adult should be present to supervise and give advice at all times in order to stimulate their creativity.

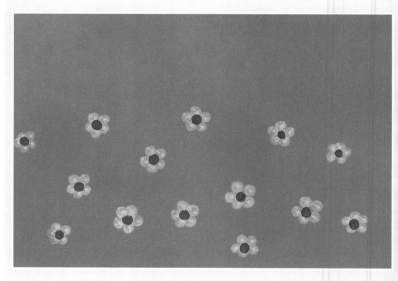

1 Make the flowers by stamping out the petals and the disk in the center with the balls of your fingers dipped in finger paint.

Which techniques will be practiced?

- *Stamping with the tips of the fingers and the sides of the hand*
- *Stamping with leaves*

3 Coat the leaves with green paint and use them to stamp trees onto the oaktag. Finish painting the trunks with your fingers.

2 With the side of your hand, stamp out the sky onto the upper part of the oaktag.

Practical Advice

- **Cleanliness:** As the children make their landscapes, they will have to clean their hands or fingers every time they change colors in order to avoid smearing the colors onto the oaktag or mixing them by accident.
- **Creativity:** The steps given here should only be used as a guideline to show how some elements in a spring landscape can be stamped; however, the children should create their own personalized landscape.

   Stamping: When stamping the tree shapes, the leaves should be softly pressed onto the paper, stroking the entire leaf to get the whole shape.

Teaching Suggestions

- *Concentrate on the characteristics and components of a* **spring landscape:** *the flowers and the names of their parts, the color of the leaves, the weather, the insects, and so on.*
- *As they use the different* **parts of their hand** *to stamp shapes, the children can learn what the parts are called, including the name of each finger.*
- *Work on the concept of* **depth and spatial orientation** *in the composition of the piece.*

5 LADYBUG 1

What materials are needed?

- Cardboard tube from a roll of toilet paper
- Red and yellow oaktag
- Black plasticine
- Four round red stickers
- Red finger paint
- Awl and felt pad or scissors
- Paintbrush
- Glue stick
- Varnish

How can the activity be done?

This activity can be done in three sessions of approximately half an hour each. The first should be done in small groups, working with one group at a time, since the activity requires active teacher supervision. The other two sessions can be done with the class as a whole.

Session 1

Prepare a table in an art corner with:
- *A dish containing red finger paint*
- *A cardboard tube for each child*
- *A paintbrush for each child (only if you have decided not to finger paint)*

1 **Paint the cardboard tube with the paintbrush or your fingers and let it dry.**

Practical Advice

- ***Plasticine:*** *Each child will need only a small amount of plasticine, since the spots they will make will be very small.*
- ***Painting techniques:*** *The cardboard tube can be painted using different methods: You can use a paintbrush or your fingers, or you can dip the tube in a dish full of diluted paint, holding it with a pair of pliers or something similar. When working with three-year-olds, it is best to finger paint.*
- ***Punching out figures in two sessions:*** *Depending on the children's age and their work rhythm, it may be necessary to allow two sessions for punching out the shapes.*
- ***Awl or scissors:*** *Use scissors for cutting out the ladybug shapes only with five- or six-year-olds in order to be sure they have good control of the scissors and can obtain good results.*
- ***Decorating:*** *The ladybugs can be used to make mobiles to decorate the classroom with spring motifs.*
- ***Making a puppet:*** *If you would like to convert the ladybug into a puppet, simply attach a stick.*

Which techniques will be practiced?

Using a paintbrush or fingers to paint • Punching or cutting out figures
Gluing cardboard and putting stickers in place • Modeling clay

Session 2

For each child, prepare:
* *The oaktag sheets with the outlines of the ladybug's body, wings, and antennae already drawn on them*
* *An awl and felt pad or scissors*

2 **Punch or cut the different parts of the ladybug out of the oaktag.**

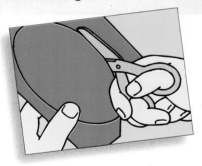

Teaching Suggestions

*Concentrate on the concepts of **over and under**.*

*Use the opportunity to practice naming the different **parts of the body** that belong to this creature and what each is for.*

*Introduce the **oval shape**.*

Session 3

For each child, prepare:
* *The cut-out ladybug parts*
* *Glue*
* *Black plasticine*
* *Round red stickers*

3 **Make small round balls with the plasticine and stick them onto the ladybug wings as spots. Varnish.**

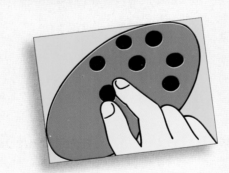

4 **Glue the front end of the red wings onto the black body so that the wing ends are free.**

5 **Glue the body onto the cardboard tube.**

6 **Glue the antennae onto the inside of the tube so they cross each other and stick out. Put the four red stickers on the ends of the antennae, two to an end and face to face.**

17

6 BUTTERFLY

What materials are needed?

- *Cardboard tube from a roll of toilet paper*
- *Green, yellow, and blue oaktag*
- *Four large blue and four large yellow round stickers*
- *Six small, red round stickers*
- *Two large red star-shaped stickers*
- *Blue finger paint*
- *Glue stick*
- *Awl and felt pad*

How can the activity be done?

This activity can be done in four sessions of approximately half an hour each, working with the entire class at one time except during the first session, which should be done in small groups of no more than six children.

Session 1

Prepare a table in an art corner with:
- *A dish containing the blue finger paint*
- *A small paintbrush for each child, unless you decide to finger paint*
- *A cardboard tube for each child*

1 Paint the cardboard tube with a paintbrush or with your finger and allow it to dry.

Teaching Suggestions

- *Concentrate on the **shape** of the circle and its **size** (large or small) and on some **spatial concepts** (on–under, above–below, front–back).*
- ***Collect photographs** of different types of butterflies and use them to complement the activity.*

Practical Advice

- ***Painting techniques:** You can use various methods to paint the cardboard tube. You can use a paintbrush or your fingers, or you can dip the tube in a dish containing diluted paint, holding it with a pair of pliers or something similar.*
- ***Decorating:** These butterflies are very decorative and could be used to add spring color to the classroom by making them into a mobile.*
- ***Making a puppet:** To turn the butterfly into a puppet, simply glue a popsicle stick to its base.*

Which techniques will be practiced?

- *Using a paintbrush or fingers to paint* • *Punching out figures*
- *Using colored stickers* • *Gluing oaktag*

Session 2

For each child, prepare:

- *The three different-colored sheets of oaktag with the outlines on them*
- *An awl and felt pad*

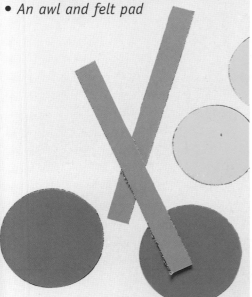

2 Punch out the shapes drawn on the oaktag (the four wings and two antennae).

Session 3

For each child, prepare:

- *The painted cardboard tube, now dry*
- *The previously punched-out shapes*
- *The colored stickers*
- *Glue*

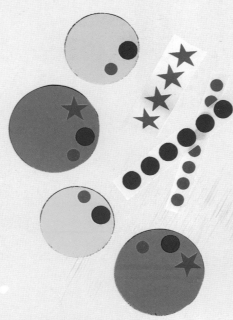

5 Put two yellow stickers on the top of each antenna end so they stick to each other also: Place the small red circles inside the yellow ones. Glue the antennae onto the inside of the tube so they cross each other and stick out.

3 Put the stickers on the four wings.

4 Paste the two green wings together so they overlap a bit. Do the same with the yellow ones.

6 Spread glue on the cardboard tube and glue on the two pairs of wings so they overlap.

7 FLOWERS

What materials are needed?

- *Orange oaktag*
- *Glossy paper in five different colors*
- *Five large round stickers of different colors*
- *Eleven large green triangular stickers*
- *Seven flat green toothpicks*
- *Awl and felt pad*
- *Glue stick*
- *Template (see page 42)*

How can the activity be done?

This activity can be done in three sessions of approximately half an hour each, working with the entire class at one time, since the activity can be easily supervised.

Session 1

For each child, prepare:
- *Sheets of glossy paper of each different color with flower outlines drawn on them, ready to be punched out*
- *An awl and felt pad*

1 **Punch out the flower shapes from the glossy paper.**

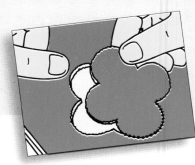

Practical Advice

- ***Toothpicks:*** *If colored toothpicks are not available, the children can color ordinary wooden ones with paint, wax crayons, or markers.*
- ***Sessions:*** *For very small children or children having difficulty keeping up with the rest of the group, two sessions may be needed to punch out all the flowers.*
- ***Gluing toothpicks:*** *When gluing the toothpicks, the children should pick them up by the tips and spread them with glue. This will require them to make an effort in order to pick up the toothpick and hold it correctly without it falling and without getting their fingers full of glue.*

Which techniques will be practiced?

- *Punching out shapes with an awl* • *Putting colored stickers in place*
- *Gluing toothpicks*

Session 2

For each child, prepare:
- *A sheet of orange oaktag with flower outlines previously drawn on it*
- *The green toothpicks*
- *Glue*

2 **Glue the toothpicks onto the straight lines drawn on the oaktag to make the stems of the flowers.**

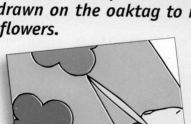

Teaching Suggestions

- *Work on naming the different **parts of the flower.***
- *Use the opportunity to concentrate on **color combinations**, since the children will have to make sure that the sticker they are going to use is a different color from that of the flower.*

Session 3

For each child, prepare:
- *The flowers punched out of the glossy paper*
- *The orange oaktag with the toothpicks glued on it*
- *The round, colored stickers*
- *The green triangular stickers*

3 **Glue the flowers onto the oaktag and put a round sticker in the center of each one.**

4 **Place the green triangular stickers along the sides of the toothpicks to look like leaves.**

8 TWO BUTTERFLIES

What materials are needed?

- Blue oaktag
- Small round red stickers
- Red, blue, green, yellow, and black glossy paper
- Glue
- Awl and felt pad
- Templates (see page 44)

How can the activity be done?

This activity can be done in three sessions of approximately half an hour each, working with the entire class at one time. Keep in mind that some children may need more time to punch out the paper parts.

Session 1

For each child, prepare:
- *Three different-colored sheets of glossy paper with the body parts of one of the butterflies drawn on them*
- *An awl and felt pad*

1 **Punch out all of the first butterfly's body parts from the glossy paper.**

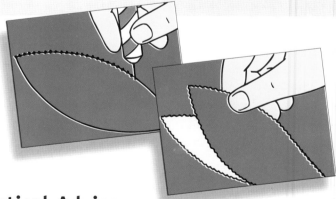

Practical Advice

- ***Working with an awl:*** *Although this activity is simple, since it only requires punching shapes out of glossy paper, it is a good idea to do it with children who are skilled at this task and aren't likely to get tired, as the entire activity revolves around using the awl. If this activity is to be done with smaller children, you will need to divide it into more sessions so they do not get tired.*

Which techniques will be practiced?
- Punching with an awl • Putting colored stickers in place
- Gluing paper

Session 2

For each child, prepare:
- Three more different-colored sheets of glossy paper with the body parts of the other butterfly drawn on them.
- An awl and felt pad

2 Punch out all of the second butterfly's body parts from the glossy paper.

Teaching Suggestions

- Take the opportunity to work on: the **shape** of the circle and its **size** (large–small), **spatial relationships** (on–under), and **direction** (downward–upward).
- Once the children finish making the butterfly, discuss the fact that the wings that were round have now visually changed shape by being covered by other body parts.

Session 3

For each child, prepare:
- A sheet of blue oaktag with the butterfly outlines drawn on it
- The cut-outs of the two butterflies' body parts
- Four round red stickers
- Glue

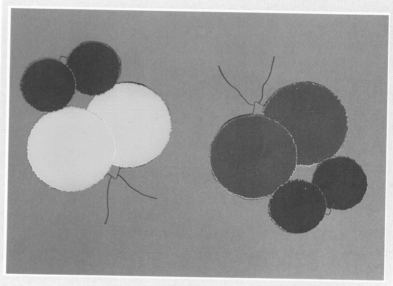

3 Glue the different wings onto the oaktag inside the corresponding outlines.

4 Glue bodies on top of wings. Place round stickers on the tips of the four antennae.

9 STAMPED PAINTING

What materials are needed?

- Blue oaktag
- Finger paint in various colors
- Small sponges
- Corks
- Potatoes cut into different shapes to make stamps

How can the activity be done?

This activity should be done in a single session of approximately half an hour, working with small groups (six children), since the children will be using a great variety of material and paint colors and the activity will therefore have to be well supervised.

Single Session

Prepare a table with:
- *Various dishes containing different-colored paint appropriate for a spring landscape*
- *A tray containing as many sponges as there are children*
- *A tray containing as many corks as there are children*
- *A tray containing potatoes previously cut into different geometrical shapes or spring motifs (butterflies, etc.) to make stamps*
- *Hand towels, paper towels, or rags to wipe hands clean*

Teaching Suggestions

- *It is important to show the children a finished piece so they can get an idea of possible results, but they **should create their own drawing** using their imagination.*
- *Allow the children to **practice stamping** on another piece of oaktag before doing the final printing.*

Which techniques will be practiced?

Stamping with potatoes • Stamping with sponges
Stamping with corks

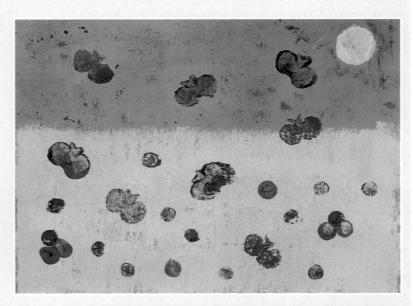

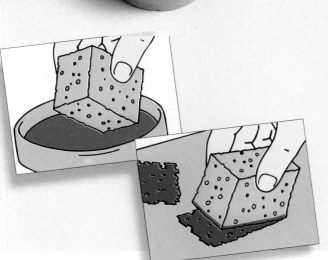

Practical Advice

• **Cleanliness:** It is very important that the children wipe their hands every time they get full of paint in order to avoid accidentally staining the oaktag.

• **One color to a stamp:** The sponges, corks, and potatoes should be used with only one color each. The children should take special care not to mix the colors by accident.

• **Overlapping colors:** If the children want to stamp an area that has already been stamped, they should wait a while for it to dry first.

10 BEAN FLOWER

What materials are needed?

- Orange oaktag
- Lentils
- Macaroni
- Green and yellow plasticine
- Glue stick
- Varnish and paintbrush
- Template (see page 43)

For a second option:
- Same as above, except substitute rice and beans for the plasticine

How can the activity be done?

This activity can be done in two sessions of approximately half an hour each, working with the entire class at one time, since the activity can be easily supervised. For the second option, a single session will be sufficient.

Session 1

For each child, prepare:
- *A sheet of orange oaktag with the outline of a flower previously drawn on it*
- *Green and yellow plasticine*

1 **Cover the circle in the center of the flower outlined on the oaktag with yellow plasticine.**

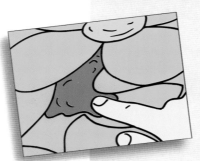

2 **Fill in the stem and leaf with green plasticine.**

Practical Advice

- ***Gluing beans:*** *It's best to spread a lot of glue on the ar[e] to be covered with beans so they stick well.*
- ***Spreading the beans:*** *To avoid getting your fingers full [of] glue, sprinkle the beans in small quantities over the area t[o] be covered and then lift the oaktag over the tray to let the loose ones fall off.*

Which techniques will be practiced?

- *Gluing beans and pasta*
- *Modeling with clay*

Session 2

For each table, prepare:
- *The sheet of oaktag with the clay on it*
- *Two trays containing lentils and macaroni*
- *Glue*
- *Varnish and paintbrush*

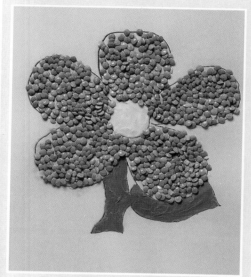

3 **Glue the lentils onto the flower petal outlines.**

4 **Make the ground out of macaroni and varnish everything.**

Alternative Option

For each table, prepare:
- *A sheet of oaktag with the outline of a flower previously drawn on it*
- *Four trays containing lentils, rice, beans, and macaroni, respectively*
- *Glue*
- *Varnish and paintbrush*

1 **Glue the lentils onto the circle in the center of the flower and the rice onto the petals.**

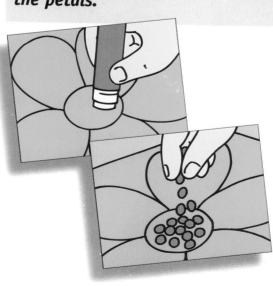

2 **Glue the beans on the stem and the macaroni along the bottom to make the ground. Varnish.**

Teaching Suggestions

- *Work on the children's **knowledge of the environment** by going over the different parts that make up a flower, how it nourishes itself, how to take care of it so it can grow, and so on.*
- *Carry out an **experiment with beans**. Place them in cotton and allow them to germinate. Watch the plants grow.*
- *Talk about the **food the children eat** that can be made from beans or pasta, allowing them to comment on their personal tastes and experiences.*

11 LADYBUG 2

What materials are needed?

- *Blue oaktag*
- *Blue and red glossy paper*
- *Black plasticine*
- *Glue stick*
- *Awl and felt pad*
- *Two large, red round stickers*
- *Template (see page 44)*

How can the activity be done?

This activity can be done with the entire class at one time, in three sessions of approximately half an hour each.

Session 1

For each child, prepare:
- *The sheets of glossy paper with the outlines of the different parts of the ladybug previously drawn on them*
- *An awl and felt pad*

1 **Punch all the body parts out of the glossy paper.**

Teaching Suggestions

- *Introduce the **oval shape.***
- *Inform the children about the **life and habits of the ladybug.***
- *Work on **spatial concepts:** on–under, above–below, on one side–on the other side.*

Which techniques will be practiced?

- *Punching with an awl* • *Gluing glossy paper*
- *Sticking plasticine to paper* • *Putting colored stickers on paper*

Session 2

For each child, prepare:
- *A sheet of blue oaktag*
- *The punched-out pieces*
- *Glue*

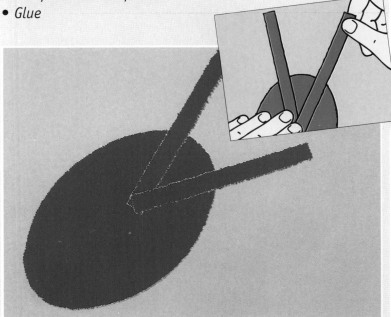

2 *Glue the glossy paper body of the ladybug to the oaktag, and then glue the antennae to the upper part of the body.*

3 *Glue the glossy paper wings on top of the body, but only at the front, leaving the back end of the wings free.*

Session 3

For each child, prepare:
- *The blue oaktag with the ladybug glued on it*
- *The two round red stickers*
- *Black plasticine*

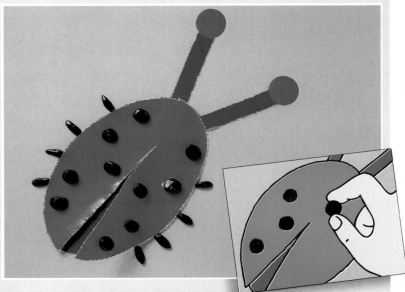

4 *Make the legs and spots with the black plasticine and stick them on by pushing a little. Then, place the red stickers on the tips of the antennae.*

Practical Advice

• ***Storing the punched pieces:*** *It is very practical to pin each child's punched-out pieces together with a clothespin in order to keep them separate for the next session.*

12 YELLOW BUTTERFLY

What materials are needed?

- Blue oaktag
- Yellow and black glossy paper
- Small round stickers: four red, four green, and six blue ones
- Glue stick
- Awl and felt pad
- Template (see pages 46–47)

How can the activity be done?

This activity can be done in two sessions working with the entire class at one time, since the activity can be easily supervised. The first session will be longer—approximately 45 minutes—the second will last about half an hour.

Session 1

For each child, prepare:
- A sheet of yellow glossy paper with the outlines of the butterfly previously drawn on it
- Round stickers of various colors
- A sheet of blue oaktag
- Awl and felt pad
- Glue

1 Punch the wings out of the glossy paper.

2 Put the colored stickers on the wings.

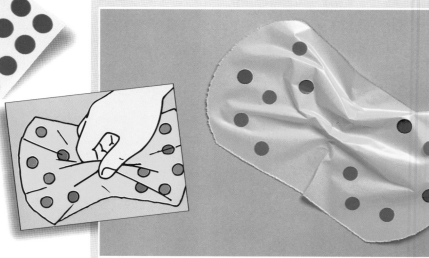

3 Glue the middle of the wings to the oaktag, wrinkling them a bit first to give them more volume.

Which techniques will be practiced?

- *Punching with an awl* • *Gluing glossy paper*
- *Using colored stickers*

Session 2

For each child, prepare:
- *A sheet of black glossy paper with the outline of the body of the butterfly previously drawn on it*
- *The oaktag with the wings glued on it and the antennae drawn on it*
- *Two small, blue, round stickers*
- *Awl and felt pad*
- *Glue*

4 Punch the body of the butterfly out of the glossy paper.

5 Glue the body over the middle of the yellow wings. Place the stickers at the tips of the antennae.

Teaching Suggestions

- *Inform the children about the **life and habits of the butterfly.***
- *Show the children a plant with the cocoons of caterpillars in the process of becoming butterflies, or bring in **silkworm cocoons,** which can be kept in a box in the classroom so the children can follow the silkworms' life cycle from the moment they hatch from the eggs until they metamorphose into butterflies.*

Practical Advice

- ***Mobile:** Another option would be to make the butterfly without gluing it to the oaktag and hang it from a string to decorate the classroom.*

13 TULIP

What materials are needed?

- *Pink oaktag*
- *Blue glossy paper*
- *Glossy paper in various colors*
- *Green tissue paper*
- *Awl and felt pad*
- *Glue stick*
- *Scissors (unless you decide to tear the paper instead of cutting it)*
- *Template (see page 46)*

How can the activity be done?

This activity can be done in three sessions of approximately half an hour each, working with the entire class at one time, although the last two sessions could be done in small groups.

Session 1

For each child, prepare:
- *A sheet of oaktag with the outline of the tulip previously drawn on it*
- *A sheet of blue glossy paper*
- *An awl and felt pad*
- *Glue*

1 **Punch the tulip out of the oaktag, leaving a hole in it.**

2 **Turn the oaktag over and glue the blue glossy paper over the hole, covering it completely.**

Practical Advice

- ***Waxed paper:*** *Waxed paper or cellophane wrap can be used instead of glossy paper. The resulting transparent flowers would be attractive decorations for the windows.*
- ***Gluing the glossy paper:*** *When gluing the glossy paper to the back of the oaktag, it is important to work with the class as a whole, especially if the children are very young, so that all the children turn over their oaktag at the same time and you can make sure they are gluing the blue glossy paper with the color side down and the blank side facing them.*

Which techniques will be practiced?

- Punching with an awl • Tearing or cutting glossy paper into small pieces
- Making balls out of tissue paper and gluing them • Gluing paper over a hole

Session 2

For each table, prepare:
- Different-colored sheets of glossy paper
- A tray on which to put the pieces as they are torn or cut

For each child, prepare:
- The oaktag with the blue glossy paper glued on it
- Glue
- Scissors (unless the paper is to be torn)

3 Cut or tear the different-colored glossy paper into small pieces and put them in the tray.

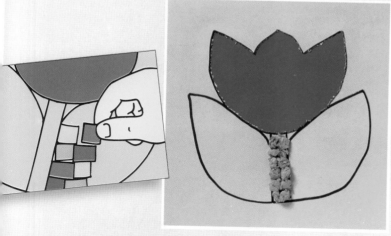

4 Spread glue onto the leaf areas on the oaktag and cover with the pieces of glossy paper to make a mosaic. Try not to leave too many blank spaces between pieces.

Session 3

For each table, prepare:
- A tray on which to place the finished tissue paper balls

For each child, prepare:
- Pieces of green tissue paper
- The oaktag with the flower and the mosaic leaves glued on it
- Glue

5 Make pea-sized balls out of the tissue paper and leave them in the tray.

6 Spread glue on the stem drawn on the oaktag and place the balls along it one by one.

Teaching Suggestions

- Plant tulip bulbs in a pot and **watch the plant grow.**
- Work on **textures** using the different types of paper used in the activity and observe the final results, such as the roughness of the tissue paper when it is made into balls.

14 YARN BUTTERFLY

What materials are needed?

- Green oaktag
- Thick yarn: yellow, green, red, and blue
- Tissue paper: yellow, green, brown, red, orange, and blue
- Large round stickers: two blue and two yellow
- Two small, round red stickers
- Glue stick
- Template (see page 45)

How can the activity be done?

This activity can be done in two sessions of approximately half an hour each, working with the entire class at one time, since the activity can be easily supervised.

Session 1

For each table, prepare:
- A tray containing the different-colored tissue paper
- Another tray on which to place the tissue paper balls

For each child, prepare:
- The sheet of green oaktag with the outline of the butterfly previously drawn on it
- Glue

1 Make balls out of the different pieces of tissue paper.

2 Spread the outline of the body of the butterfly with glue and cover it with the tissue paper balls from top to bottom without leaving any empty spaces.

34

Which techniques will be practiced?
• *Gluing yarn* • *Putting on colored stickers*
• *Making and gluing tissue paper balls*

Session 2

For each table, prepare:
• Three trays containing the yarn cut to the appropriate sizes according to color
For each child, prepare:
• The oaktag with the finished body of the butterfly
• The colored stickers
• Glue

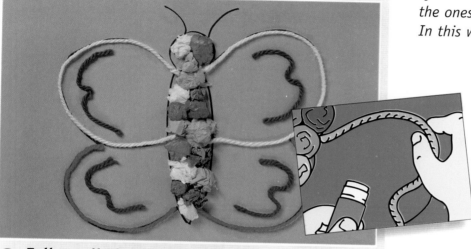

3 Follow all the outlines of the wings with the glue stick and glue the yarn on.

4 Put the large stickers on the wings, two above and two below. Then finish off the antennae by placing the two small stickers on their tips.

Teaching Suggestions

• *This activity works on **pre-writing skills** by having the children follow lines.*
• *Several **pre-mathematical concepts** can be worked on here: length (long, medium, and short), lines (open and closed), and size (large and small).*

Practical Advice

• ***Free composition:*** *You can give the children a great variety of colors and thicknesses of yarn so they can freely choose the ones they like the best, and the same with the stickers. In this way, each finished piece will be more individual.*

15 ANT

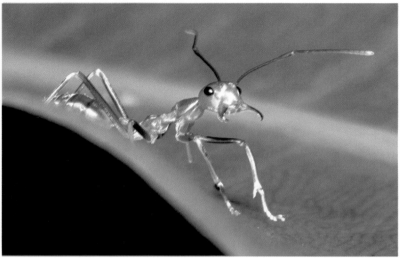

What materials are needed?

- Yellow oaktag
- Coffee beans
- Black and red plasticine
- Black wax crayons
- White glue
- Template (see page 47)

How can the activity be done?

This activity can be done in three sessions of approximately half an hour each, working with the entire class at one time, since the activity can be easily supervised.

Session 1

For each child, prepare:
- *A sheet of yellow oaktag with the outline of an ant previously drawn on*
- *A black wax crayon*
- *A piece of red plasticine*

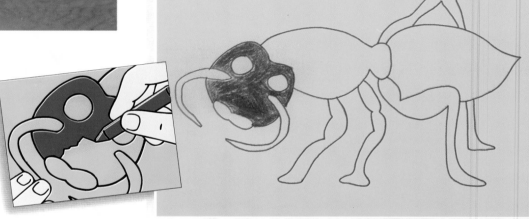

1 **Color the ant's head black with the wax crayon.**

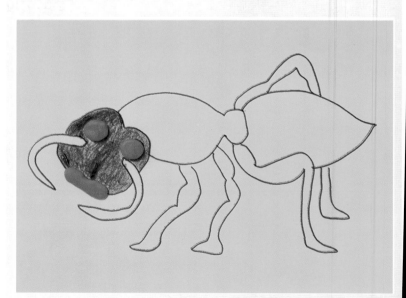

2 **Make the eyes and the mouth of the ant with the red plasticine.**

Which techniques will be practiced?

- Coloring with wax crayons • Modeling plasticine
- Gluing coffee beans

Session 2

For each table, prepare:
- A dish containing coffee beans

For each child, prepare:
- A tube of white glue
- The oaktag with the finished face

3 Spread the glue generously on the body of the ant and glue the coffee beans in place one by one.

Session 3

For each child, prepare:
- A piece of black plasticine

4 Make six sausages with black plasticine and stick them onto the oaktag to make the legs and antennae. Push hard to make sure they stick.

Practical Advice

- **Plasticine:** The children should only be given a small amount of plasticine to make the eyes and mouth. This makes it easier for them to distribute the amounts well.

Teaching Suggestions

- Give the children information about the **life and habits of ants.**
- Show the children a **prefabricated ant nest.**
- Work on the **color black.**

16 GIFT BOX WITH FLOWER

What materials are needed?

- Red, yellow, and green plasticine
- Red glossy paper
- Large matchbox
- Varnish and paintbrush
- Awl and felt pad
- Glue stick

How can the activity be done?

This activity can be done in three sessions of approximately half an hour each, working with the entire class at one time, since the activity should be well supervised.

Session 1

For each child, prepare:
- *The red glossy paper with a rectangle the size of one side of the matchbox drawn on it*
- *An awl and felt pad*
- *Glue*

1 **Punch the rectangle out of the sheet of glossy paper and glue it onto the matchbox.**

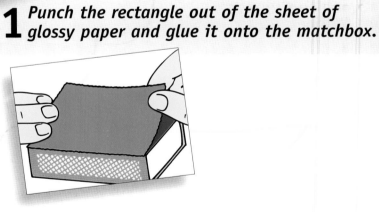

Practical Advice

- ***Utility:*** *The matchbox can be used to store small things.*
- ***Directing the activity:*** *The process of making the plasticine flower should be directed step by step. Although it only consists of making balls, if it is not followed well, the results could be disappointing.*
- ***Cleanliness:*** *Every time the children change plasticine colors, they should wash their hands to avoid mixing them.*

Which techniques will be practiced?

- Punching with an awl • Gluing glossy paper
- Modeling with plasticine • Varnishing

Session 2

For each child, prepare:
- Pieces of red, yellow, and green plasticine

2 To make the petals, form five balls of yellow plasticine about the size of a pea and flatten them so one end is somewhat pointy, and the other rounded.

3 Make a slightly bigger ball out of red plasticine and flatten it to make the center of the flower.

4 Make two balls out of the green plasticine of about the same size as the red one and flatten them into a leaf shape.

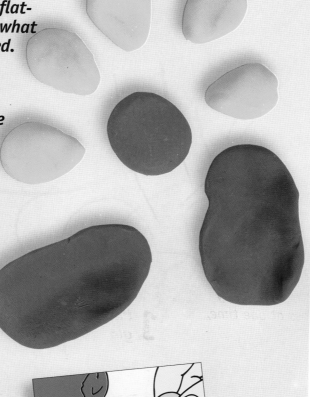

5 Stick the petals onto the center one by one, then stick the leaves onto the back of the flower.

Session 3

For each table, prepare:
- A dish containing varnish

For each child, prepare:
- The box with the glossy paper glued on it
- The plasticine flower
- A paintbrush

6 Stick the flower on the box and varnish it generously so it remains in place.

Teaching Suggestions

- Name and observe the **parts of the flower.**
- Work on **volume.**

17 WALL TILE WITH FLOWER

What materials are needed?

- Blank white floor tile
- Permanent black marker
- Yellow, green, red, and orange plasticine
- Varnish and paintbrush
- Template (see page 48)

How can the activity be done?

This activity can be done in two sessions. The first should last approximately half an hour, working with the entire class at one time. The second will be shorter and should be done in small groups (four to five children).

Session 1

For each child, prepare:
- *A white floor tile with the outline of a tulip previously drawn on it with a permanent marker*
- *A piece of plasticine of each color: yellow, green, red, and orange*

1 **Fill in the bottom of the tile with yellow plasticine, shaping it with your thumb.**

2 **Fill in the stem and leaf with green plasticine.**

Teaching Suggestions

- *Talk about **wall tiles:** where the children have seen them before, what they are for, and so on.*
- *Tell the children all about **tulips.***

Which techniques will be practiced?

- *Modeling with clay*
- *Varnishing*

3 *Make the flower with red plasticine.*

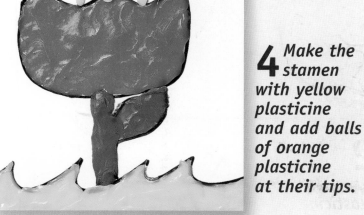

4 *Make the stamen with yellow plasticine and add balls of orange plasticine at their tips.*

Session 2

Prepare a table in a varnishing corner with:
- *A dish containing varnish*
- *A paintbrush for each child*
- *The wall tiles created during the last session*

Prepare another table with:
- *Newspapers on which to place the varnished tiles to dry*

5 *Varnish the plasticine part of your tile and leave it to dry.*

Practical Advice

Supervising the activity: It is important to supervise the activity to avoid having the children fill in one part of the tile before another or mixing colors.

- *Plasticine: The plasticine to be used should be distributed in the right quantities so that each child does not have too much left over. Distribute only the color being used at the moment.*

- *Varnishing: Only the plasticine should be varnished, using the varnish sparingly.*
- *Decoration: These tiles can be hung like paintings or placed upright on a table with a support.*

41

TEMPLATES

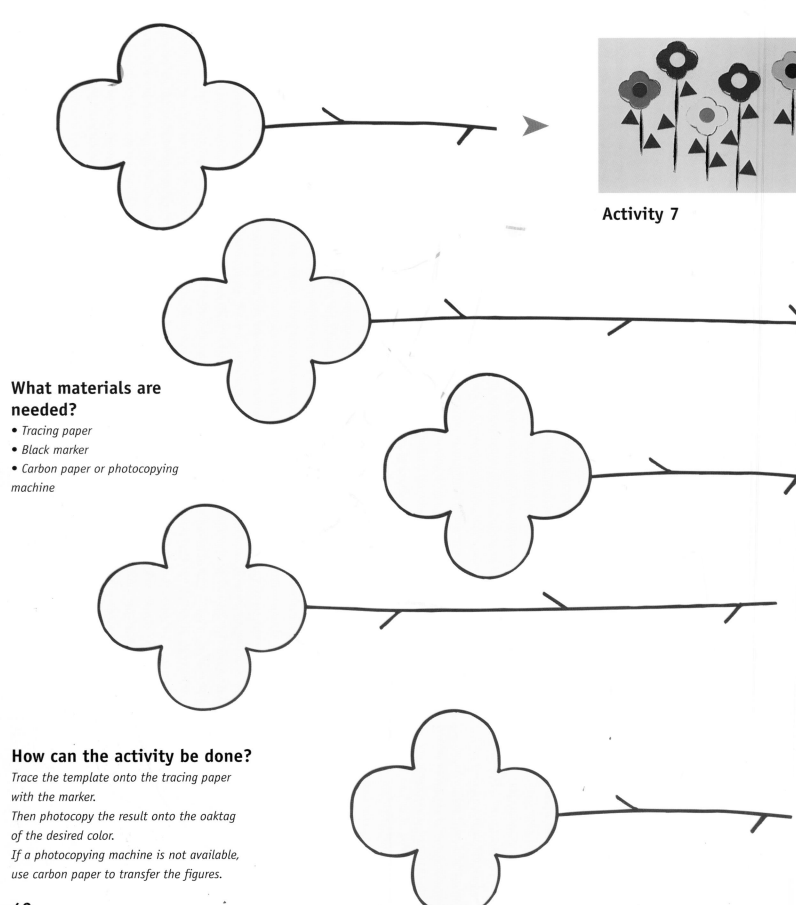

Activity 7

What materials are needed?
• *Tracing paper*
• *Black marker*
• *Carbon paper or photocopying machine*

How can the activity be done?

Trace the template onto the tracing paper with the marker.

Then photocopy the result onto the oaktag of the desired color.

If a photocopying machine is not available, use carbon paper to transfer the figures.

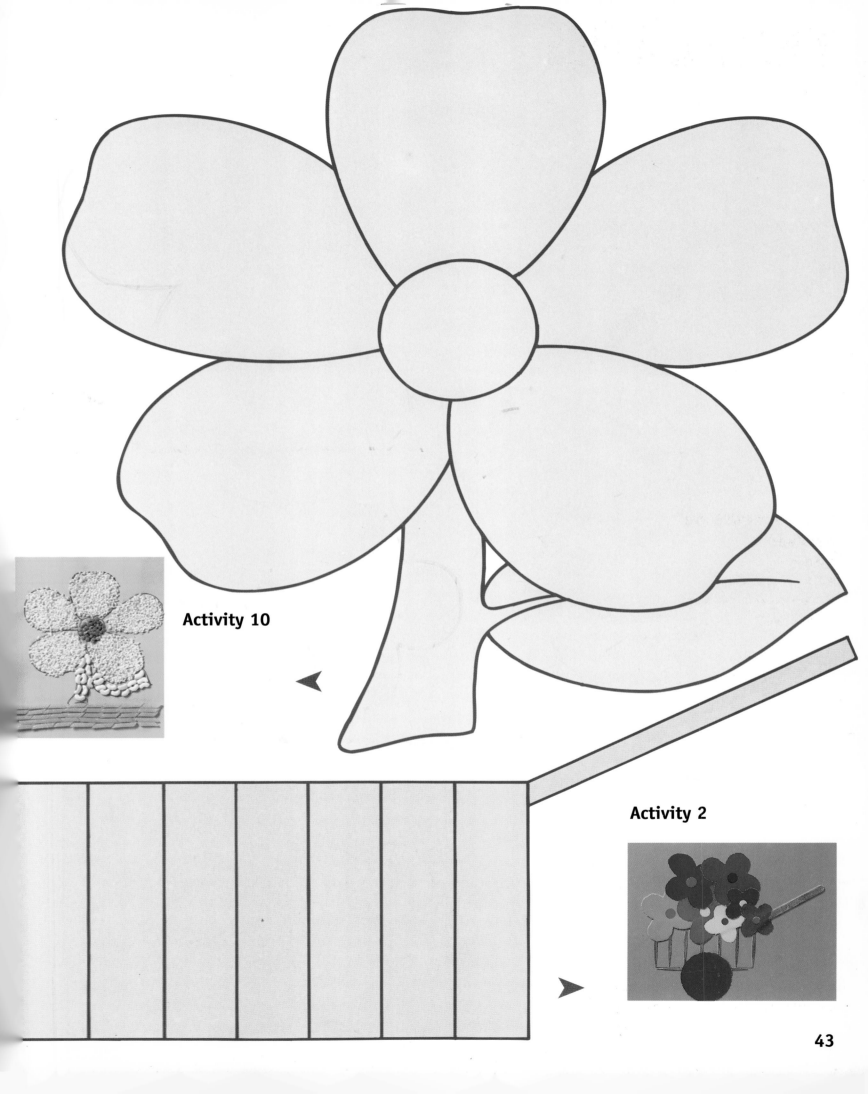

Activity 10

Activity 2

TEMPLATES

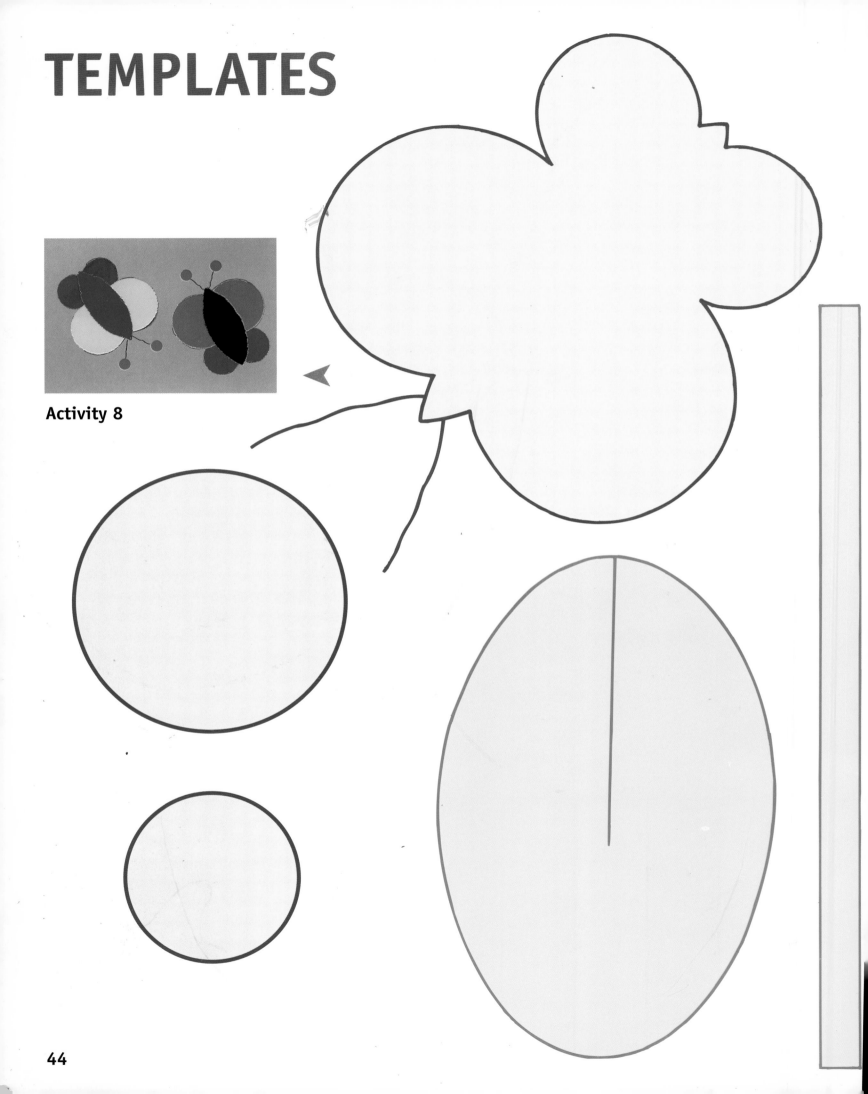

Activity 8

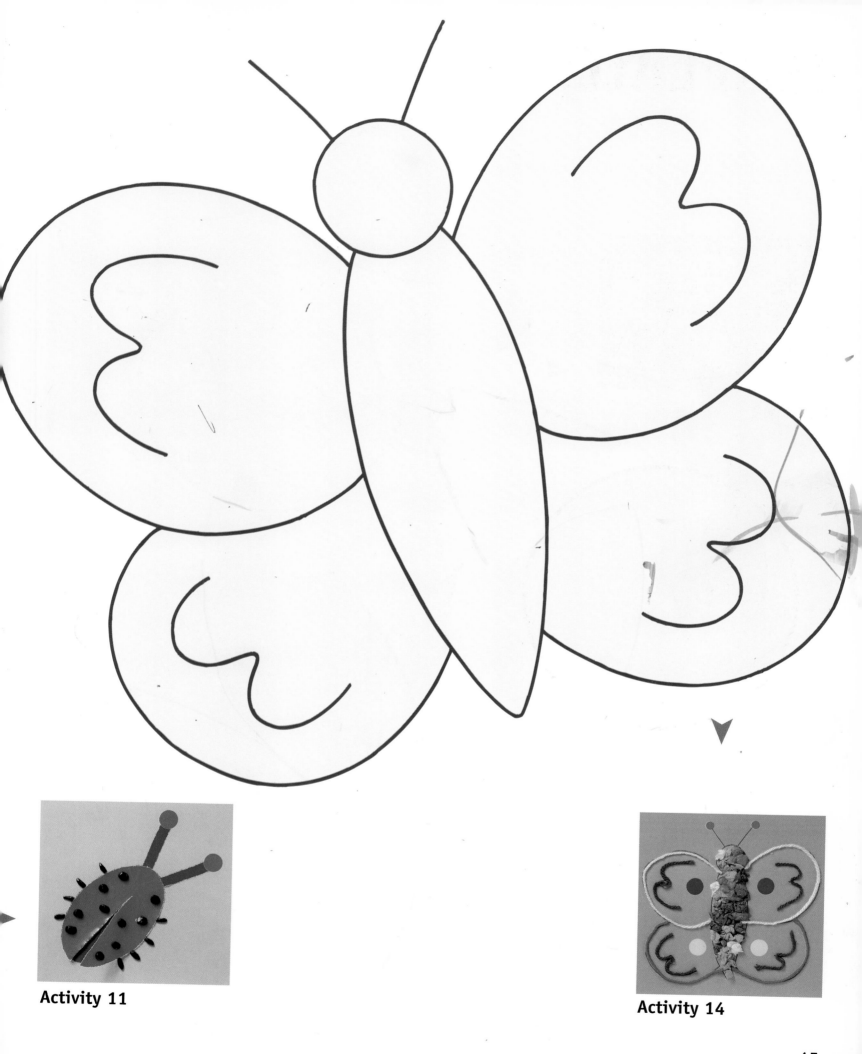

Activity 11

Activity 14

TEMPLATES

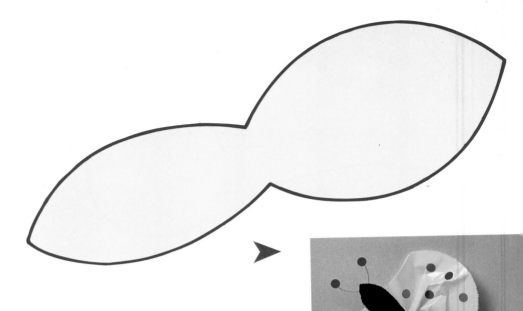

Activity 13

Activity 12

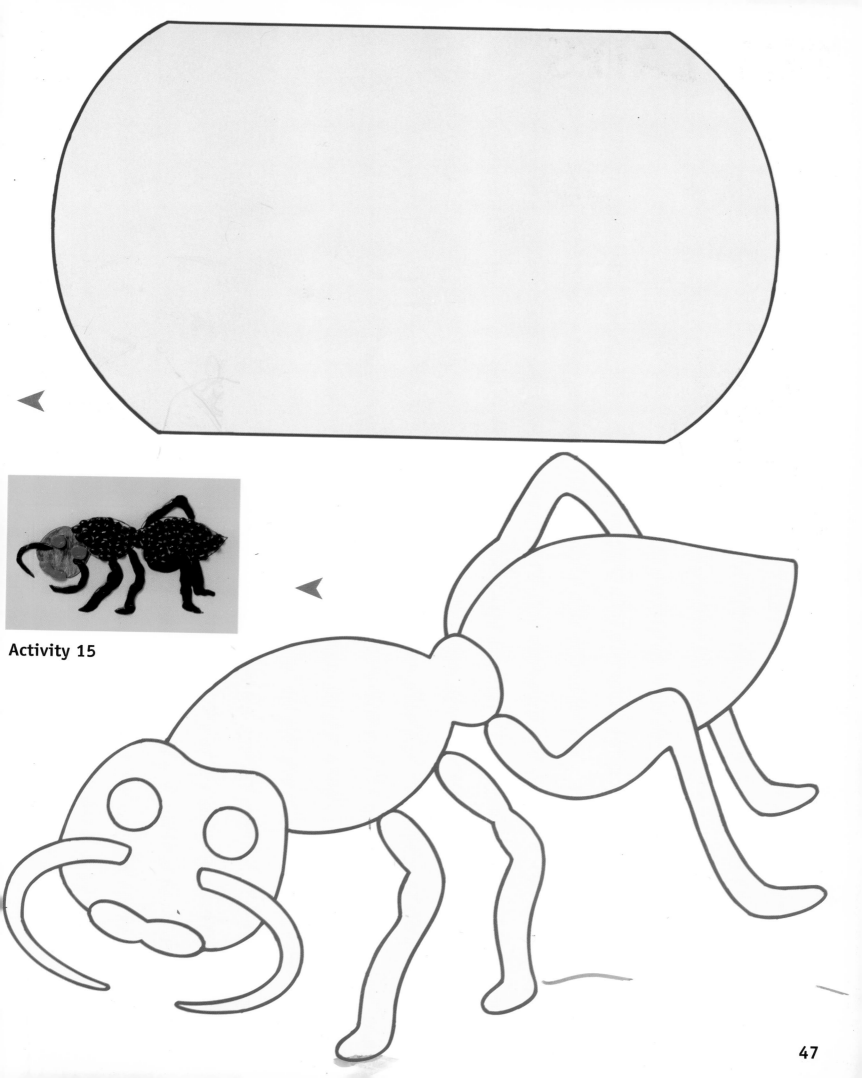

Activity 15

TEMPLATES

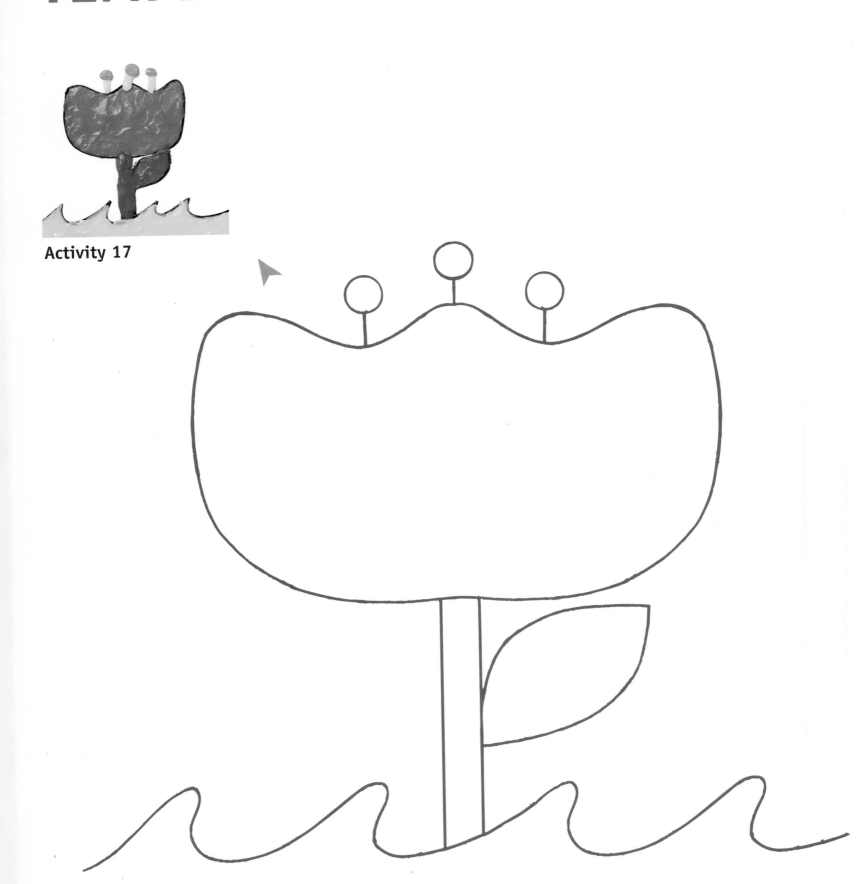

Activity 17